Juan and the Jackalope

A CHILDREN'S BOOK IN VERSE

Rudolfo Anaya

Illustrations by
Amy Córdova

UNIVERSITY OF
NEW MEXICO PRESS

ALBUQUERQUE

15 14 13 12 11 10 09   1 2 3 4 5 6 7

Library of Congress Cataloging-in-Publication Data

Anaya, Rudolfo A.

Juan and the jackalope : a children's book in verse / Rudolfo Anaya ; illustrations by Amy Córdova.

   p. cm.

Summary: Competing for the hand of the lovely Rosita and her rhubarb pie, Juan rides a jackalope in a race against Pecos Bill.

ISBN 978-0-8263-4521-9 (hardcover : alk. paper)

[1. Stories in rhyme. 2. Pecos Bill (Legendary character)—Fiction. 3. Animals, Mythical—Fiction.

4. New Mexico—Fiction. 5. Tall tales.] I. Córdova, Amy, ill. II. Title.

PZ8.3.A5298Ju 2009

[E]—dc22

2008054127

Book design and type composition by Melissa Tandysh ⚘

Composed in 15/22 Zephyr Regular ⚘   Display type is Zephyr Regular

⚘ Printed and bound in China by Oceanic Graphic Printing, Inc.

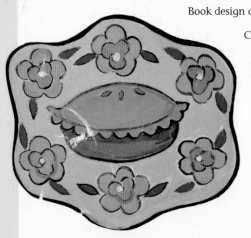

Mythical creatures appear in the stories of many cultures. In New Mexico, one of our most interesting magical creatures is the Jackalope, which is a jackrabbit that has antelope or deer horns. When I was a child, my uncle Juan told me that long ago he caught a Jackalope near the village of Puerto de Luna. He and the Jackalope went on many adventures. In my mind I could see my uncle and the Jackalope flying through the sky, over the river, and up to the moon. The stories my uncle told me made my imagination grow and grow.

I dedicate this book to my uncle and all the wonderful storytellers of New Mexico.

—Rudolfo Anaya

To Viletta Munro Sprangers, my precious mother, with all love and gratitude.

And to the new day . . . may it unfold in glorious blossoms of delight, wonder, and possibility!

—Amy Córdova

Listen, my children,
and I'll tell you a tale;

You can read it now
or check your e-mail.

This happened in the future
—long ago,

In the magical land
of New Mexico.

This cuento is 'bout
the Great Grasshopper Race

And the prize Rosita
awarded first place.

Rosita, the loveliest gal
in the Pecos River Valley,

Sang like a coyote
with a thorn in its belly.

She wore a ten-gallon hat
and rode an armadillo;

It took her ten years
just to get to Amarillo.

She said, "I'll bake a rhubarb pie
for the winner,

And serve it with frijoles
and ice cream for dinner."

A thousand vaqueros
vowed to win or to die;

All loved Rosita
and her delicious pie.

But they had no chance
against Pecos Bill;

He rode Hoppy,
a grasshopper
big as a hill!

Bill bragged, "I'll finish
in the bat of an eye,

And claim Rosita
and her delicious pie."

My tío Juan
was just a young
buckaroo,

But with a glance
from Rosita
his love grew
and grew.

"I can't win the race,"
Juan howled and cried,

"I don't have a burro
or nothin' to ride."

His tears gushed
and flooded the river;

His moan made La Llorona
shake and shiver.

The Crying Woman said,
"I know who can beat Bill;

That's Jack the Jackalope
from Unicorn Hill.

Grab my hand, niño,
and we'll speed away

To a land where
dragons dance all day.

You might see the Kookoóee
and a fancy troll

Eating rhubarb pie
as they take a stroll."

So off they went
through the starry night,

Crossed el río
in the purple moonlight.

It was strange indeed
to see dragons dancing

And find the Kookoóee
laughing and prancing.

"Have I gone mad?"
a puzzled Juan cried.

"Nope, you're in Texas,"
La Llorona replied.

"Here's the Jackalope
who will help you win;

Hop on, muchacho,
and go for a spin."

Juan got on Jack
and away they went;

They landed in New Mexico
in a circus tent.

Pecos Bill smirked,
"Can that poor thing run?

Beating you
will be a barrel of fun!"

The Jackalope trembled
as he looked around;

It seemed no one loved him,
but he stood his ground.

"Let Bill ride first,"
said Rosita,

"I'll go bake a pie
in my casita."

Pecos Bill shouted, "Giddyup!"
and Hoppy took off,

Over the Rockies, Dallas,
and the Juárez bluff.

He cleared El Paso,
flew over Santa Fé,

Crossed the Río Grande
and landed okay.

The grasshoppers cheered—
it was quite a thrill.

"Try topping that!"
bragged Pecos Bill.

The animals laughed
when Juan got on Jackalope;

His chances, they thought,
were thin as smoke.

Rosita didn't laugh,
she knew Juan would try.

She winked and whispered,
"Remember my pie."

"I'm ready," said Juan,
adjusting his sombrero.

He sat in the saddle
like a true caballero.

He smiled at Rosita
with love in his eyes,

"Don't forget the tacos
and a bag of French fries."

Then off they flew
    in a marvelous motion,
Crossing right over
    the Atlantic Ocean.

Over Africa, España,
    Italy, and France,
The Jackalope did
    a toe-tapping dance.

They cleared Mt. Everest
on the way to the moon
And cruised by the Dipper
singing a tune.

Juan held fast
   to the horns of his steed,

Waved his hat and shouted,
   "¡Ajua!—Yes, indeed!"

   They flew far beyond
      the world that we know,

   Whistling at planets
      all neat in a row.

They stopped for shakes
at the Milky Way

And finished all this
in less than a day.

When the Jackalope finally
turned back to Earth,

He streaked like a falling star
filled with mirth.

They landed with a thud
near Santa Fé,

And no one doubted
they had won the day!

Stardust clung
to the daring pair;

It sparkled on their clothes
and tangled hair.

Everyone cheered
when Rosita kissed Juan
And gave him the pie
he had bravely won.

Juan asked Rosita,
"Will you be my bride,
And ride on the Jackalope
by my side?"

"I'll marry you
and ride by your side,
Rich or poor
I'll be your bride.

Fly to the moon
and the star-filled sky.

We'll dine on beans
and rhubarb pie."

♥ The End ♥